Kitty Crowther is part-English, part-Swedish and lives in Belgium. Winner of the prestigious Astrid Lindgren Memorial Award, her work is influenced by the wonderful books she had as a child.

Pippa Curnick was a book designer before becoming an illustrator. She's an avid reader, walker, and biscuit lover, and is also a whiz at puppet- and model-making.

Gerda Dendooven is a celebrated Belgian illustrator, author, and occasional actor. She uses pencils, ink, and collage to make her humorous, expressionistic pictures.

Michael Foreman is one of the UK's most acclaimed illustrators. He has illustrated over three hundred books, and has travelled around the world from the Arctic to the South Pacific to research them.

Lucia Gaggiotti likes to express joy, happiness, and fun in her pictures. She says that drawing children's books lets her step inside the page and live in that world.

Thank y[illegible] illustrators who donated their work for free in aid of the Three Peas charity.

Ingrid Godon loved drawing more than any other school subject. She writes her own books, too, and especially likes drawing poetic, sensitive pictures of people and places.

Susanne Göhlich is a much-loved German illustrator. Her many books feature lots of people, every animal you can imagine – and ten very adventurous ghosts!

Chris Haughton grew up in Dublin but has lived all around the world, from San Francisco to Kathmandu. His quirky, brilliantly colorful books have won him international acclaim.

Nicola Kinnear is an illustrator, storyteller, and maker of beautiful things (she's especially good at crochet). She loves to bring magic, nature, and folklore into her books.

Library of Congress Cataloging-in-Publication Data available

ISBN 978-1-338-62705-3

10 9 8 7 6 5 4 3 2 1 20 21 22 23 24

Printed in Malaysia 108

This edition first printing, August 2020

In conjunction with publishing this book, a donation has been made
to Three Peas, a charity that gives vital practical help to refugees.

Kind

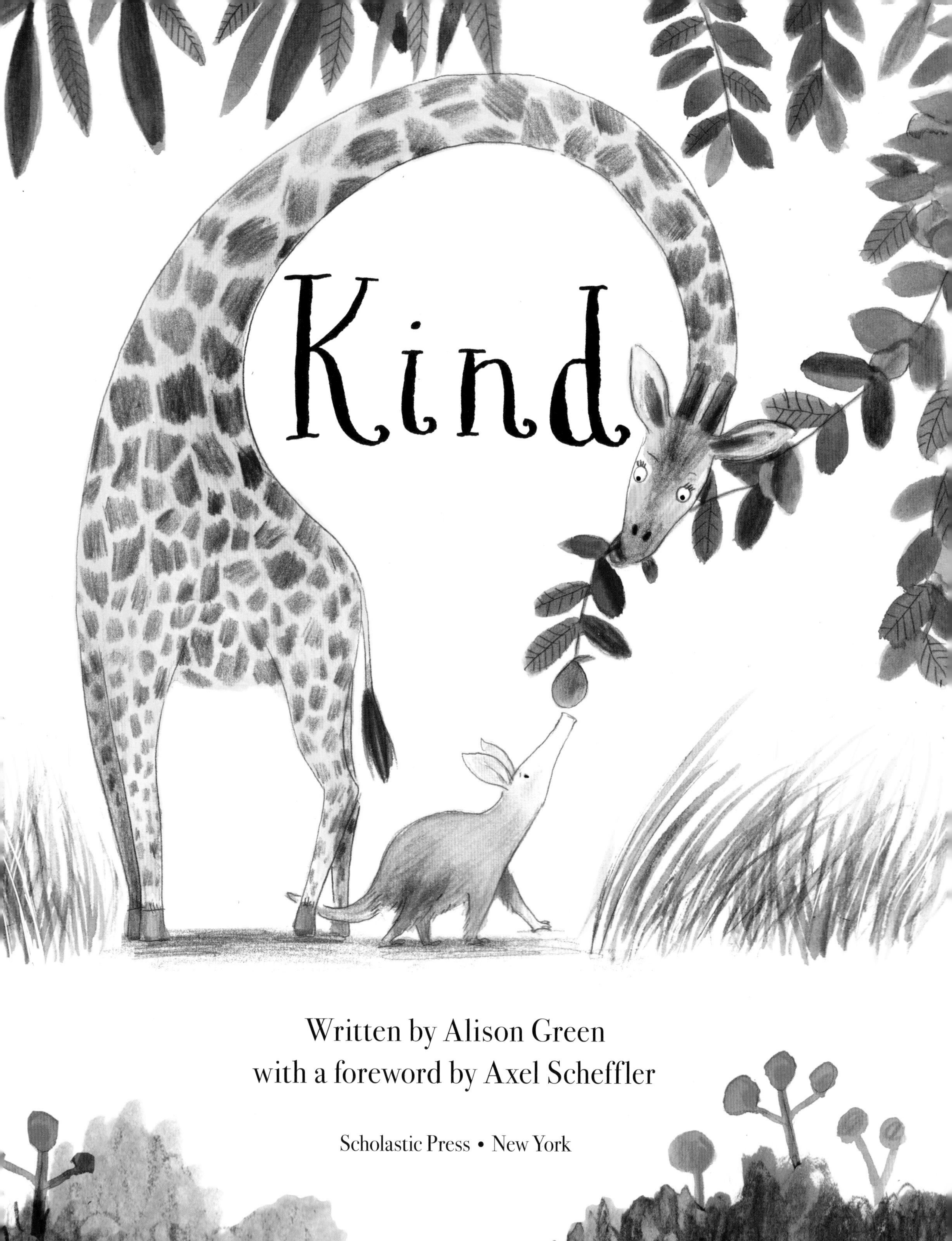

Written by Alison Green
with a foreword by Axel Scheffler

Scholastic Press • New York

What can you do to be kind today?

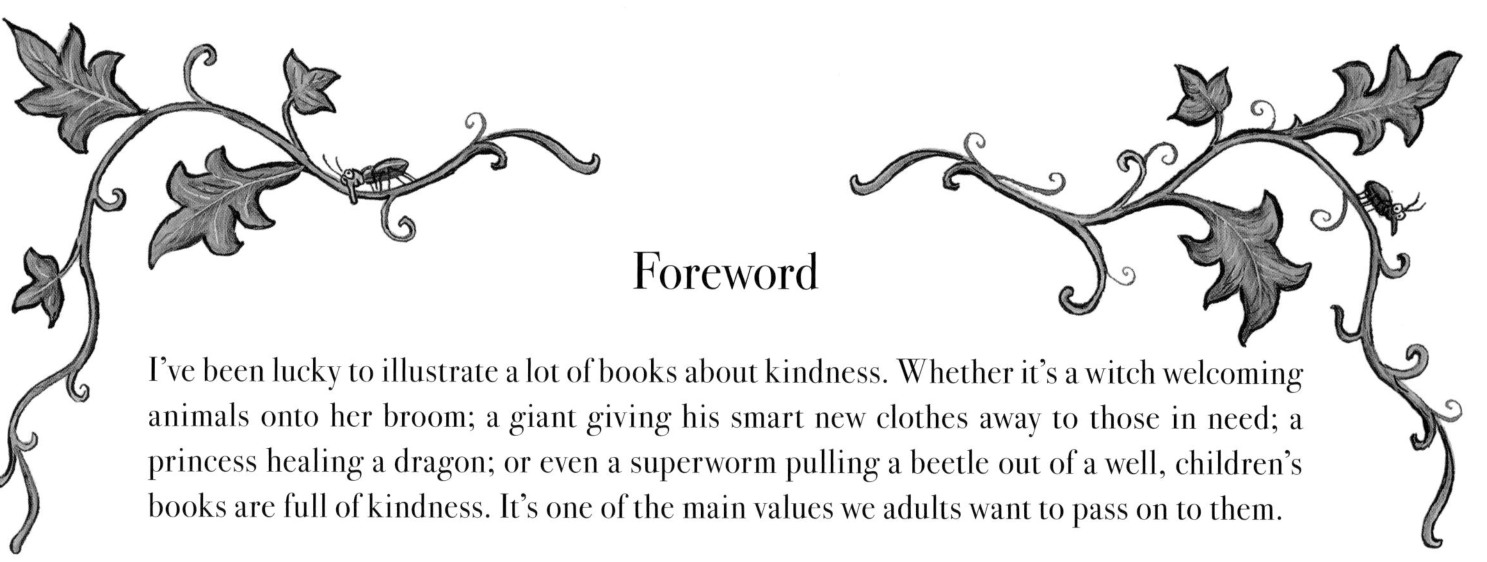

Foreword

I've been lucky to illustrate a lot of books about kindness. Whether it's a witch welcoming animals onto her broom; a giant giving his smart new clothes away to those in need; a princess healing a dragon; or even a superworm pulling a beetle out of a well, children's books are full of kindness. It's one of the main values we adults want to pass on to them.

Whether it's the small acts of kindness that brighten our daily lives, or the bigger questions of how we help those in real need, we know that a kinder world is a better world.

But sometimes it feels as if we're just too busy to stop and give a hand to those who need it. Sometimes we feel helpless, as if nothing we do will make enough of a difference. It's good to remind ourselves that even the smallest acts of kindness really can make an impact.

The world seems full of division at the moment, but I believe passionately that it's only by being kind, generous, open, and compassionate that we'll make a peaceful, prosperous world for the next generation.

I have been a patron of the Three Peas charity for over two years and have seen how much of a difference small acts of kindness can make to those who are in desperate need. Three Peas is a charity that has helped make a difference in the lives of many refugees in the most desperate circumstances, and I'm proud to be supporting their vital work.

I hope that both children and adults will enjoy exploring this book. It's full of amazing illustrations by many of the world's top illustrators, who have all donated their work for free. The images they've created are joyful, funny, moving, and inspiring. They feature monkeys, elephants, lions, cats, dogs, worms — and even people! And they show us many simple ways in which we can all help to make the world a better place.

Axel Scheffler

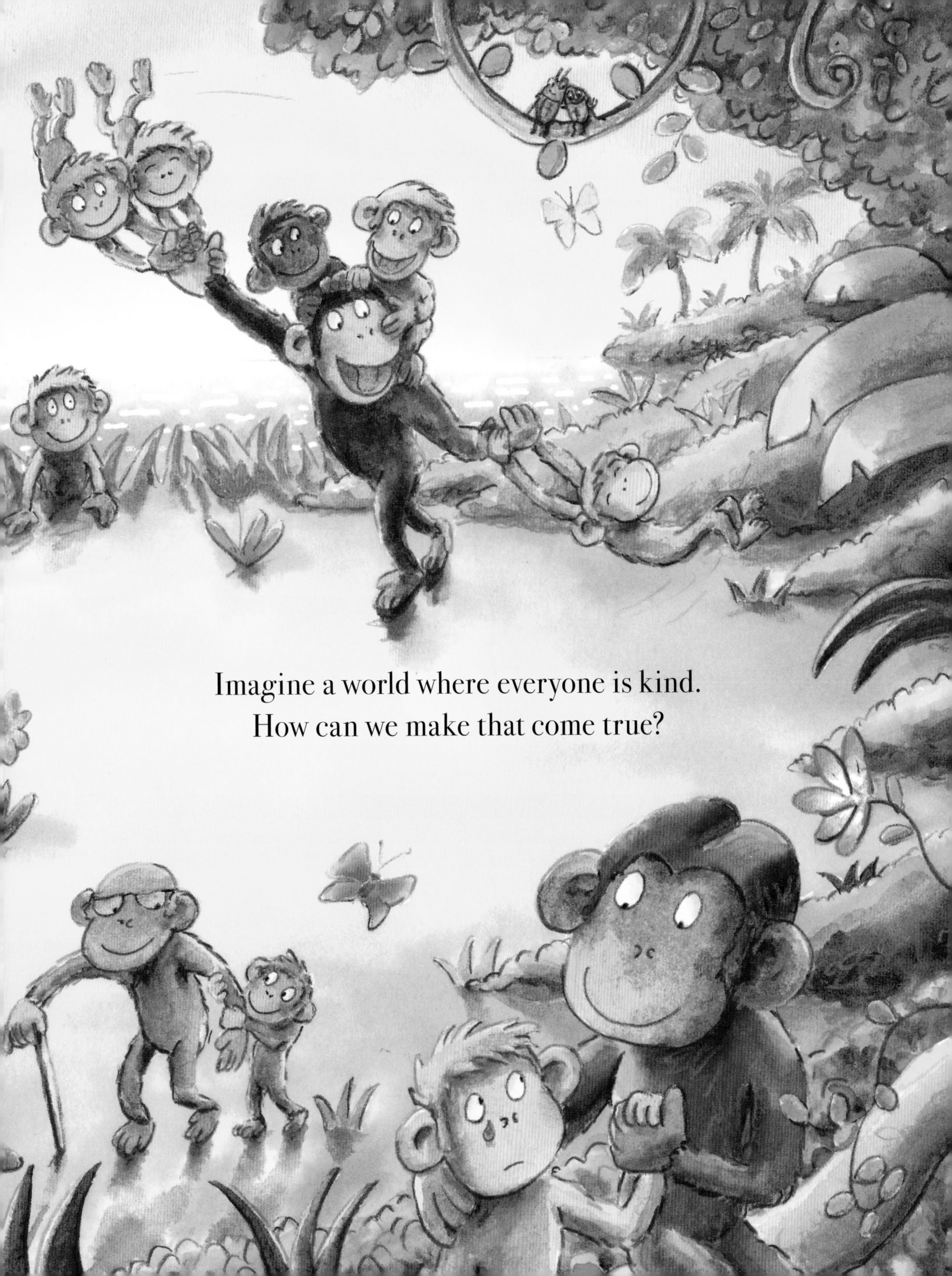

Imagine a world where everyone is kind.
How can we make that come true?

Here’s a good place to start —

just give someone
a smile!

There are lots
of good ways
to be kind.

We can listen to people,
especially when they're sad.

We can give them a hug
if they're feeling lonely.

If someone's frightened or worried,
we can offer to hold their hand.

If they're in trouble, we can see if we can help.

Can you tell someone
a story to cheer
them up?

It's good to listen to
their stories, too.

And let's make sure
no one's left out when
we're playing a game

and that everyone
is cared for.

Have you ever made
a Kindness Jar?

Every time you do something kind,
put a marble or a button into it.
I bet you'll soon fill it up!

What else can you do to be kind today?
Here are some good ideas.

Can you help carry a bag?

Or pick up things people have dropped?

Or let someone else
go in front of you?

It's really kind to be patient —
especially when you don't feel like it!

Animals need lots of kindness, too.

What do you do best?

We're all good at different things,
so let's give everyone the chance to shine.

Sometimes extra kindness is needed,
such as when you meet someone
who's new where you live.
Can you be a good friend
and help them feel
at home?

What's their
favorite game?

Is it a quiet one?

Or a really noisy one?

If they're trying to learn our language, perhaps you can tell them new words?

How about learning some words from their language, too? Look at all these different ways of saying "Hello!"

CIAO
WITAJ
KON'NICHIWA
Привет
Czesc
Ni hao
Sah-wahd-dee!
Üdvözlöm
ciao
Olá
HELLO
HOLA
CIAO
HALLO
Marhaba
Hujambo
Salut
Hej
Bog!
Haloo
NAMASTE
Shalom
Tēnā Koe

Sometimes people have lived through very hard times. They've had to leave their homes and their countries because of danger.

They are brave and amazing and have extraordinary stories to tell.

How can you welcome them?
Can you share your toys
with them?

Or draw pictures
together?

Sometimes people say
we don't have enough to share,
and there's no room for anyone
more. But maybe you can say,
"There's plenty of room!
Come on in!"

After all, if you don't let people in, you'll never know what you're missing. There might be a wonderful new friend just outside the door.

Everyone is valuable,
and we all have gifts to share.

Let's be curious about the world
and all the people in it.

It’s fun to see what we do the same

and what we do differently.

Everyone can be kind,

even if they're really small
or a bit shy.

It feels nice to be kind.
And it's a good idea, too.
Because if everyone is kind . . .

. . . we'll make a better world.

Three Peas – Help make a difference!

In conjunction with publishing this book, a donation has been made to Three Peas, a charity that gives vital practical help to people who have had to flee their homes.

It takes a lot of courage to leave your home, to leave everything behind, and to travel to another country, but that's what many people around the world are forced to do.

There might be a war where they live and their homes are no longer safe. Or they might come from countries where they're not allowed to live the way they want to, or say what they want to, or practice their religion. They feel they have no choice but to leave and find a safer place to live.

They have to make long, difficult, dangerous journeys. When they finally arrive in their new countries, they have to apply for permission to stay — a process that can take years. During that time, it's hard for families to find work or even somewhere to live.

That's where organizations like Three Peas can lend a hand. They may help people find a home, and can provide basic supplies of clothes, food, and all sorts of essential items from shampoo and toothbrushes to books and strollers.

After so much upheaval, families long for a bit of normality. They want to cook food together and celebrate their feast days. They want to learn the local language. They want to work and support their families, and they want their children to have a good education.

Many people have skills that they used in their old lives that they're keen to use again. They may be doctors, teachers, lawyers, or artists. Some of the people that Three Peas have met have volunteered as math teachers and translators. Others have gone on to make a living as hairdressers, restaurant owners, jewelry designers, and even sculptors.

Three Peas helps run a center where people can take language classes, receive advice, and make friends. They even helped three little girls find an after-school dance class, which really helped them settle into their new country.

As people learn the language of their new country, and their children go to school, they can start to make safe, new, happy lives for themselves.

Three Peas was started by a group of friends from six different countries.
They are a small organization but have achieved an amazing amount. As they say:
"Imagine if every single one of us did something small to help? Together we could make a big difference!"
You can find out more about Three Peas at threepeas.org.uk.

Thank you to all the kind illustrators who donated their work for free in aid of the Three Peas charity.

Lydia Monks is the award-winning illustrator of the What the Ladybird Heard series by Julia Donaldson. She has a poodle called Chadwick who likes to distract her while she's working.

Ole Könnecke has received many awards for his illustrations. Born in Germany, he grew up in Sweden, and his style of drawing owes a lot to the comics he loved as a child.

Jörg Mühle is a German illustrator who creates irresistible pictures of rabbits, penguins, bears, and many more. He is quite tall and has an awful lot of dots on his name.

Anke Kuhl likes to draw pictures with a dark sense of humor (she even has a couple of little skeleton models on her desk). She also likes to relax by cooking or playing the piano.

Thomas Müller illustrates stunning theater posters as well as beautiful children's books. He lives in Leipzig and enjoys walking in the woods and collecting classic cars.

Sarah McIntyre has illustrated books featuring everything from Dinosaur Firefighters and Jampires to Cakes in Space. She loves dressing up and owns lots of dramatic hats.

Barbara Nascimbeni is an Italian-born illustrator who creates richly colored pictures. She lives in Germany and France and also enjoys gardening and playing the accordion.

Dorothée de Monfreid created a host of entertaining dogs for her books *A Day with Dogs* and *SHHH! I'm Sleeping*. Based in Paris, she also loves to write and draw comics.

Guy Parker-Rees is the acclaimed illustrator of *Giraffes Can't Dance* and *Dylan*. He has drawn and doodled all his life, loves cake, and has his best ideas when sitting under a tree.